MW00899560

MAKING GREAT CHOICES!
History of Economic Thought for Youths
(& Other Individuals More Interested in Dogs than Economics)

Volume 1: Trade & Labor Economics

Briggs & Dan Jones

This book is the first of a series. Volume 2 will cover topics more relevant to the field of Public Economics. We are very grateful for expert feedback from the Owen-Palmer household.

It was Monday morning.

Poppy & Luka had a problem...

They would like to go to Grandma's house on Friday to play with Bea and Joyce...

... but, they cannot go until they do all of their chores.

"Every morning, we get a letter with our chore list.

If we do all our chores for four days, we get to go to Grandma's house.

Today, we need to fold socks and set the table."

"SO MUCH TO DO!

We are STUCK and don't even know where to start!

We'll NEVER get to Grandma's house..."

Poppy & Luka were overwhelmed by their tasks.

Luckily Uncle Dan had a great idea!

"Well, we could look at what some famous economists say. After all, economics is the study of making choices, so maybe that will help you think about where to start!"

Let's look at the very first economist... Adam Smith.
He lived in Scotland and wrote books almost 250 years ago.

Here was his big idea:

When there are two jobs that need to be done and two people, if each person works on the job they are best at, they'll finish sooner than if they both work on both jobs!

*That's **specialization!***

"So, that means if I set the table and Luka folds the socks we could get our chores done faster!"

"LET'S DO IT!"

THE NEXT DAY: Tuesday morning.

"Today, we need to load
the dishwasher and
pick up all of our clothes.
Luka, which will you do?"

"But, um, Poppy is faster at both of those. If we work on the stuff we're good at, like the Scottish guy said, does that mean Poppy does everything this time?"

"Actually, the economist David Ricardo has an answer for that! Let's hear from him."

*You can still benefit from working on different jobs, even if one person is better at both! If one person is really good at one job, just make sure they're doing that one. That's called **comparative advantage!***

THE NEXT DAY: Wednesday morning.

"Hey Luka, today we have to wash clothes and clean the floor. But, great news! For these jobs, I have some machines!

I have a vacuum cleaner for cleaning floors, and a washing machine for washing clothes.

How about this? You can use my machines to do chores! That way we are both specializing -- just like Ricardo and Smith said."

"Great! It will go so much faster!

But, what will you do while I vacuum and clean the clothes?

What is your job?"

"I am going to sit in my hammock & drink lemonade.

My job is *owning* the machine. Your job is *using* the machines.

Totally fair! I bet all the economists would say so!"

"Totally UNFAIR!

And not all economists would agree!

Karl Marx and Friedrich Engels said..."

"I think that means I need to revolt against Poppy and take all of her machines!

Where's my water pistol?"

"I don't think Marx or Engels would support you being so tough on your sister...

... and maybe we can turn to another economist to make Poppy think differently about this.

Let's hear from Thorstein Veblen. You know, he was a Minnesotan! Maybe Veblen has a good idea!"

With some people doing all of the work, and some people just taking in the rewards, the group getting the rewards starts focusing too much on showing off how much they have. The problem is, that doesn't help the group as a whole get their jobs done!

And Poppy realized...

"My neighbors, the Carnegies and the Fricks, will always have better monocles and top hats than me...

I'm tired of trying to keep up with them. Maybe laying in my hammock, watching Luka work, isn't making me happy after all.

I think I will work alongside Luka. With our machines and both of us working, we could get done *even* faster."

Luka & Poppy finished washing clothes and cleaning the floor together, and went to bed.

While they slept that night, several feet of snow fell to the ground!

THE NEXT DAY: Thursday morning.

"We have a big problem! The sidewalk is covered in snow and the mail lady can't get to our house to bring us the mail. She can't deliver our last chore!"

"What are we going to do? We just had to do one more chore before we could go to Grandma's house! Without that letter, we'll never get to go!"

"Well, that is tricky! But there is one more economist to hear from, John Maynard Keynes. Let's see if his ideas can help!"

People used to think that a lack of jobs would fix itself. That's not always true! Sometimes you need a helpful hand to get things started again.

How stimulating!

"How about this?

If I give you guys shovels, you can shovel the sidewalk.

That can count as your last chore *and* you'll be able to get letters again in the future when you get back from Grandma's house."

"GREAT IDEA!"

"WE'RE GOING TO GRANDMA'S HOUSE!"

I'm really glad we heard about these economists. I wonder what the next great economist will think of!

CPSIA information can be obtained
at www.ICGtesting.com
Printed in the USA
LVHW020929210120
644250LV00012B/650